BIG
BROTHER,
LITTLE SISTER

To His Royal Highness O.A. Sijuwade, The Ooni of Ife,
who showed me considerable personal kindness during my stay in Nigeria.
And to Ms Cheryl Wright who was my guide and introduction into Yoruba society.
E ṣe — I. T.
To Gwen and Bert, Eva and Jinky. And for Kevin — J. C.

Barefoot Books
37 West 17th Street
4th Floor East
New York, New York 10011

This book is printed on 100% acid-free paper
This book was typeset in bold Goudy Sans ITC 16pt on 26pt leading
The illustrations were prepared in colored paper collage

Graphic design by Design/Section, England
Color separation by Bright Arts, Singapore
Printed and bound in Hong Kong by South China Printing Co. (1988) Ltd.

1 3 5 7 9 8 6 4 2

U.S. Cataloging-in-Publication Data   (Library of Congress Standards)

Thomson, Ian.
   Big brother, little sister / written by Ian Thomson ;
illustrated by John Clementson.—1st ed.
[40]p. : col. ill. ;   cm.
Summary: An adventurous young elephant finds herself alone
and afraid in the darkness of the African jungle—until a friendly
mouse comes to her rescue.
ISBN 1-84148-117-3
1. Individual differences —Fiction. 2. African elephant—Fiction.
I. Clementson, John. II. Title.
  [E]—dc21 2000 AC CIP

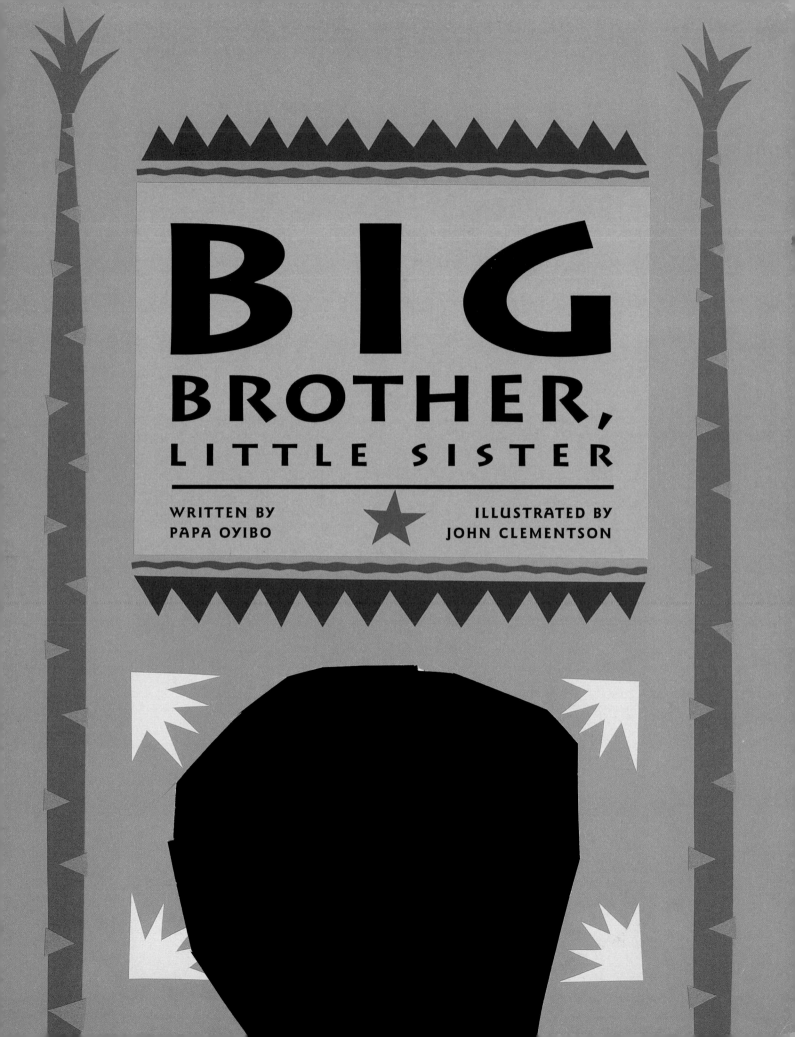

BIG
BROTHER,
LITTLE SISTER

WRITTEN BY
PAPA OYIBO

ILLUSTRATED BY
JOHN CLEMENTSON

FOREWORD

Throughout my life, I have had the good fortune to spend time living in other people's exciting and interesting countries. During my two-year stay in Nigeria, I became a regular visitor to the Court of His Royal Highness, the Ooni of Ife. I also traveled through the country, going out into the villages in the late afternoon, when the day's work was done, to sit in the shade and meet the people who lived there. My visits to the Royal House and to the villages of the plains and jungle enabled me to gain many insights into the traditional culture, myths and legends of the Yoruba people.

The Yoruba have a rich oral tradition. In speech, story, song and dance, they perf___ f___ tales of the creation time, animal f_____ _d mortals. Somewhe_____ere is a platform _____ _ low wall buil_____ anopy of broad _____ ers from bot_____ ches, stools and _____

If you sit down under this canopy, you will be offered cold beer or some cola. If you wait a little longer, the children will come; the "small dash" follows, where you present a gift of a sugar sweet to each child. Then the adults will arrive, joining you at the tables around the platform.

Now is the time that the exchange can begin, each person telling the stories that they have brought to the "Circle of the Dance." If you are fortunate enough to sit within the circle, you too will be expected to participate in the storytelling. If chosen, you will become a performer, entertaining the assembled group with your words. As darkness falls, the oil palm lamps are lit and the bonds of a common brotherhood are built through sharing tales of magic, adventure and friendship.

This is how I became a storyteller in the land of Africa. The story that follows is the first of the many tales that I told, which earned me the name "Papa Oyibo" ("the elder who is a white man").

Ian Thomson

Once upon a time, there was an elephant and a mouse.

They lived in a land called Africa, where the sun shines,

the rain falls, and the trees grow. This is the story of
how the elephant and the mouse became friends.

The elephant lived with her mother, her aunts and
her sisters, in a very large family, for that is the custom
of the elephants in the land of Africa. And, as is the

way of all elephants, they traveled every day, trekking
far across the land.

One day, when the elephant and her family were
eating at the edge of the forest, she saw the most
beautiful flowers, just a little way farther into the trees.

She looked around carefully, for she knew that her mother did not want her to wander off on her own. But the flower-trees were so beautiful and she thought it could do no harm.

And so, when she was sure that no one was looking, she slipped into the trees and through the jungle toward the place where the flower-trees grew.

When she came to the place of the flower-trees, the elephant reached up with her trunk and, breathing gently through her long nose, smelled the most wonderful smell in the world: the smell of honey-butter and hot cookies.

"Mmmmm! Wonderful...wonderful..." said the elephant as she ate all of the first flower-tree, for that is what elephants do.

But, of course, eating one flower-tree is just like
eating one cookie. If you eat one, then you have to eat
another, and another, and another!

The elephant went from tree to tree, moving farther and farther into the jungle, eating all the flower-trees she could find.

Suddenly it was dark, and the elephant was alone, and the elephant was afraid. For in the land of Africa, the darkness of the night comes as quickly as the blink of an eye.

She didn't know what to do, for she had never been
alone before, and in the deepest darkness, the jungle
came alive with the sounds of the night. Bats flew.
The snakes slithered, and the crocodiles crunched on
the bones of the dead.

The elephant was afraid, so she ran and ran into
the darkness of the night. She couldn't see where she

was going, smashing through the jungle, scattering
trees and bushes everywhere, until, at last, she ran

into a thorn-bush.

A giant thorn stuck in her foot and she crashed to the ground. She was alone, crying in the darkness, and she could not move.

Meanwhile, the mouse who lived in a very small hole at the bottom of a very big tree was having a quiet doze, dreaming of juicy fruits, hard nuts, and a soft warm bed.

Suddenly he was awakened by a thunderous roar. The earth shook, the tree trembled, and his store of nuts fell clatter-batter around his head.

"Wa'H Allah!" said the mouse, as he scrambled outside. "What's happening?" Then he looked up, and he saw and he said, "A mountain has fallen from the sky."

Then a blast of sound — like the roar of a thousand trumpets — thundered from the mountain.

The noise sent the mouse tumbling backward and he

was about to run when he heard a small voice crying,
"Help me! Help me!" coming from somewhere near the
other end of the mountain.

"Don't worry, I'm coming," said the mouse. "I'll save you! Don't panic." But then he saw a big, wriggly thing lying beside the mountain.

"Snake! Snake!" he cried as he screeched to a halt.
(For in the land of Africa, the mouse is a favorite dinner
of the snake.)

"Where, where?" cried a terrified voice, as the
mountain leapt into the air.

"There," said the mouse in astonishment. "It's stuck

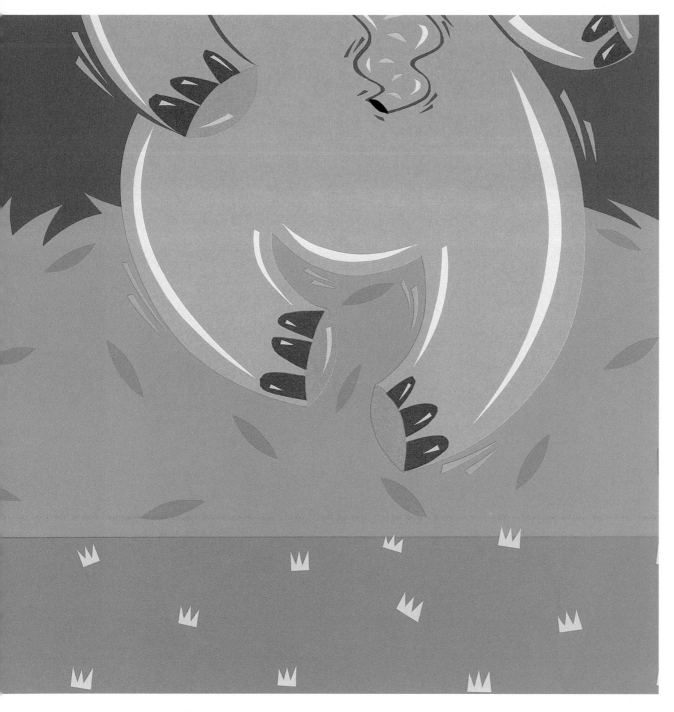

on you."

"Aaaaah!" cried the mountain. "I hate snakes." And
it waved its trunk to shake off the snake.

"Oh!" said the mouse, looking at the biggest moving thing he had ever seen. "It's not a snake — it's part of you. What is it, and what are you?"

"I'm an elephant," said the mountain, "and that's my trunk."

"How very interesting," said the mouse. "I've never seen an elephant before, or a trunk. You're very, very big," said the mouse. "In fact, you're gigantic."

"And what are you?" asked the elephant.

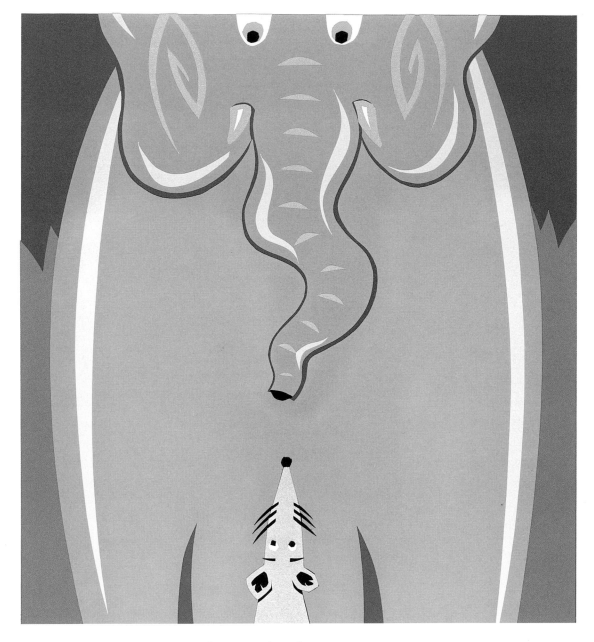

"I'm a mouse," he replied.

"Well," she said, "I've never seen a mouse before. You're very, very small. In fact, you're tiny."

"That's true," said the mouse, "but *I'm* not the one that's crying. What's wrong? And how can I help you?"

Then the elephant told him her story, and all the time she was telling it, tears ran from her eyes as she tried again and again to pull the thorn from her foot with her trunk.

"Don't cry," said the mouse. "Don't cry! I can help you!"
With that, he ran up the elephant's left leg, and gripped
the thorn between his teeth and paws.

Harder, then harder and harder he pulled until at last, with a mighty heave, the thorn came free, and the elephant cried with joy. The pain had gone.

"Thank you, thank you," said the elephant. "You have saved me. Please tell me your name."

"My name?" said the mouse. "I don't have a name."

"What do your family call you?" asked the elephant.

"I don't have a family," said the mouse. "I'm alone."

"Oh, how sad," said the elephant. "No one should be alone. I will be your sister," she said, "and I will give

you a name. You will be called 'Te Te Oka,' which means 'my big brother who is very small.'"

The mouse laughed, puffed out his chest and was very proud, for the giving of a name is a great thing and it is a gift of great power. But the giving of any gift requires a return gift of equal importance.

"Then," said the mouse, thinking very carefully, "if I am your big brother, you must be my little sister, so my naming gift to you will be your name, 'Tu Tu Eloka,' which means 'My little sister who is very big.'"

"Thank you for such a beautiful name," said the elephant. "You have given me the gift of life and the gift

of a new name. But what can I do now? It's dark, and I
don't know where I am, and I have lost my family."

"Don't worry, little sister," said the mouse. "I will
protect you. You can sleep safely here tonight, and
tomorrow we will look for your family. Lie down," he
said, "and I will sleep on your curled-up trunk."

She lay down and laughed because it tickled when
the little mouse snuggled into her trunk, and in laughing
she forgot her fear.

And so they slept, two friends, the biggest and
smallest of all the animals in the forest. And when they
awoke, the sun was shining, and the trees were growing.

And big brother mouse and little sister elephant
laughed, because they were friends.

walk
the way of wonder...

Barefoot Books

The barefoot child represents the person who is in harmony
with the natural world and moves freely across boundaries of many kinds.
Barefoot Books explores this image with a range of high-quality picture books
for children of all ages. We work with artists, writers and storytellers from many
traditions, focusing on themes that encourage independence of spirit,
promote understanding and acceptance of different traditions,
and foster a life-long love of learning.

www.barefoot-books.com